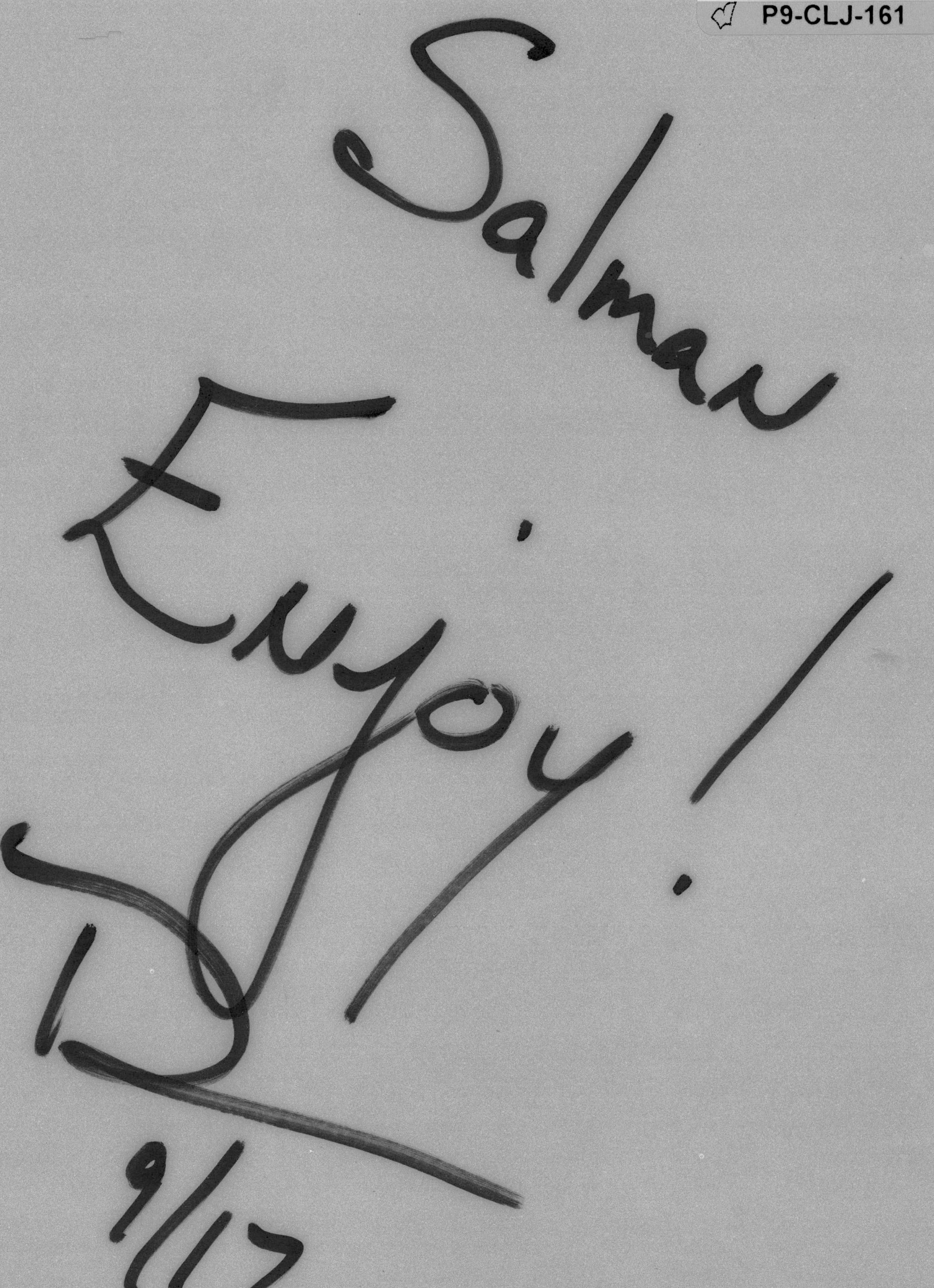
Salman
Enjoy!
9/17

Salman

Enjoy!

Adoption Is...

By D. A. Royster

Illustration by: Karen V. Penn

At school Michael and his class were learning about families and he asked the question
" Do you know what ***Adoption Is***...?"
When no one raised their hand to answer his question, Michael began telling them his adoption story.

for
at
is
me
the
one
my
3+0=
1+1=
2+1=
Aa
Bb
Cc
9
3
6
Families
Morning Schedule
9:00 Circle Time
9:30 Reading
10:00 Snack
10:15 Recess
11:00 LUNCH
Our Pets

He said,
" Adoption was a wonderful experience
that happened to me." He told the class that
he does not live with his birth mommy and daddy.
Michael said, "***Adoption Is...*** Foster Families."
Those are families that you live with for a little while.

He said, " ***Adoption Is...*** Social Workers."
They are the people who look for
families for you to be part of.

Adoption Is... Po - ten - tial Family Visits.
Potential means: maybe.
So those are visits with "Maybe Families."

Michael said, "***Adoption Is***... moving day."
That means the Social Worker brings you
to live with your new family.

Michael told the class, "***Adoption Is***...
when he and his new family went
to a place called a Courtroom.
There was a man there named
Judge who sat at a

big

big

B...I...G...

desk and all the grown ups signed papers to make
us family forever and ever".

Exit
Clerk

For Michael, ***Adoption Is***... a Daddy,

a Mommy,

Holy Bible
Apples
Sailing
The Best Stories

brothers and sisters,

Playing
Chess

a Grandma and Grandpa,

aunts, uncles and cousins.

Blueford
Family Reunion
44
CHIPS

Adoption Is... a special place
just for him.

DB
My Favorite Book

He said, "***Adoption Is***... lots of love and

a church family to love you, too."

worship church

Michael said, “Adoption was a
wonderful experience that happened”
to him.

This labor of love would have never been possible without my Heavenly Father's guiding light and the support of family and friends.

Thank you to:

* My parents for teaching me to love and live life.
* My brother for his sense of humor and gentle spirit.
* Grandma for teaching me to believe.
* Karen for unbelievable strength.
* Numerous friends and family for patience and listening ears.

A very special thanks to Darryl, Ebonie and David for continued unconditional love and support.

To My Wonderful Son,
Words could never describe the joy you bring.
Love,
Mom

"In all thy ways acknowledge Him, and He will direct thy path."
Proverbs 3:6

Library of Congress: 2004090037
ISBN: 0-9761538-0-7

Published by Unspeakable Joy Press
For information or to place an order contact us at:
Unspeakable Jot Press
P. O. Box 252
499 Adams Street
Milton, MA 02186

E-mail us @ www.adoptionis.com